1

Milly at Magic School

Dedicated to Annette,
for her spiritual help and inspiration

First Published in Great Britain in 2003
by Piccadilly Press Ltd.,
5 Castle Road, London NW1 8PR

Designed by Louise Millar

Printed in Hong Kong
for the publishers Piccadilly Press Ltd.,
5 Castle Road, London NW1 8PR

ISBN: 1 85340 752 6 (paperback)
1 85340 757 7 (hardback)

1 3 5 7 9 10 8 6 4 2

Set in Aunt Mildred 24pt

A catalogue record of this book
is available from the British Library

Jane Andrews has two sons and lives in High Wycombe in Buckinghamshire.
Since graduating from art college, she has illustrated a variety
of graphic work, including illustrations for magazines.
She has written and illustrated five books for Piccadilly Press,
including the four books in the highly successful Zoe series:

ISBN: 1 85340 640 6   ISBN: 1 85340 651 1   ISBN: 1 85340 644 9   ISBN: 1 85340 726 7

MiLLY at Magic SCHOOL

Jane Andrews

Piccadilly Press • London

Today was Milly's first day at Magic School and she was really excited. She had worked very hard to pass the entrance exam – Magic School wasn't easy to get into!

Mrs Marsh, the Head Mistress, was waiting at the front door to greet the children.

Ms Divine, Milly's new teacher, introduced her to the class and said that Milly was a 'star pupil'.

Most of the children staring back at Milly were smiling, except for three girls in the front row, Prunella, Beatie and Floe.

They started to pull faces. Why should *they* want a 'star pupil'
in *their* class?

When the lessons began, strange things started to happen to Milly.
First, her pen wouldn't write. Nothing appeared on the paper! She
tried three different pens and a pencil, but none of them worked.
Ms Divine noticed. "This is odd, Milly. Why don't you try the
blackboard instead?"

But the chalk went completely out of control when Milly picked it up.
"Dear me, this sort of behaviour won't do," said Ms Divine,
thinking it was all Milly's fault.
Milly saw Prunella, Beatie and Floe laughing at her. She felt
embarrassed and cross.

The next day was even worse. Just before lunch, Milly's hair suddenly stood straight up in the air. And it started to grow upwards right in front of everyone's eyes!

And then her tunic turned bright pink.

"Something is very wrong here," said Ms Divine to Milly.

"I think you'd better see the school nurse at once."

Milly sat down in the nurse's chair feeling very low.
"Hmm, I think someone has been playing magic tricks on you,"
said the nurse.
Milly was too shocked to say anything, but then she thought of
Prunella, Beatie and Floe.

"Your tunic will go back to blue soon, but I'll just go and get something special for your hair," said the nurse, very kindly. While she was gone, Milly looked around the room. It was full of jars, bottles and books. She saw that one large book was lying open.

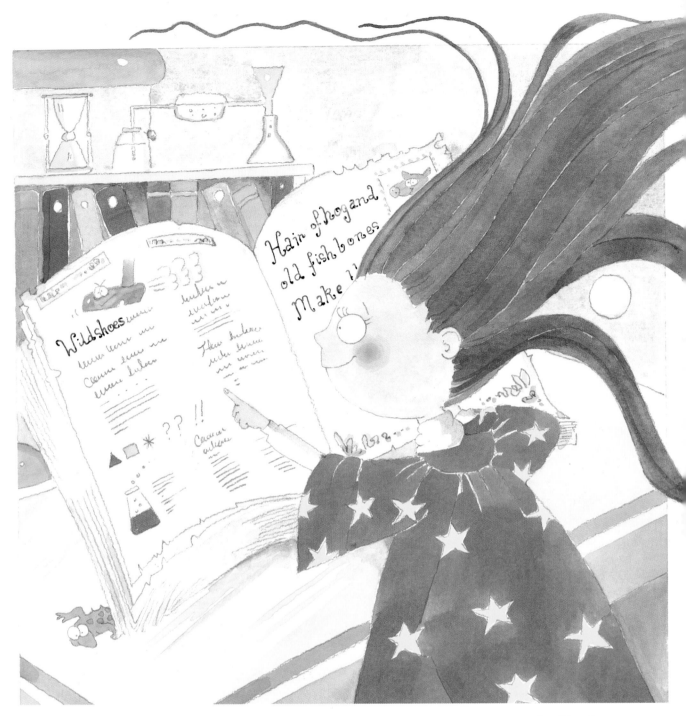

Milly carefully turned the pages of the book. It was full of
magic potions! She suddenly remembered Prunella, Beatie and
Floe laughing at her.
"This could come in handy," she thought.
She found one called "Wild Shoes" and memorised it. Then she
quickly shut the book as the nurse returned.

Milly had to drink a terrible-tasting potion, but, thank goodness, her hair turned back to normal!

Back home, Milly thought and thought about the spell. Where could she get hair of hog? When she patted her dog Dido she suddenly knew what to do.

She mixed up the potion using dog's hair, not hog's hair, and fish food instead of old fish bones.

Milly decided to try the spell out on her fish, Sven, just to be safe. She put a pinch of the potion in the goldfish bowl.
"Make this fish have a mind of its own!"
Poor Sven! He jumped out of his bowl, wiggled up the wall and somersaulted, and then plopped back down into his bowl.
"Wow!" said Milly.

Next day when everyone was ready for gym, Milly carefully sprinkled some of her potion into Prunella, Beatie and Floe's gym shoes. They were too busy talking to notice anything.
"Hair of hog and old fish bones,
Make these shoes have a mind of their own,"
whispered Milly.

Everyone was working hard at their stations, when suddenly there was a lot of noise.

Prunella, Beatie and Floe stumbled across the gym floor. "Help!" screeched the three girls as they spun, whirled and rolled around.

FIZZ!

BANG!

POP!

went their gym shoes.

Eventually the shoes ran out of steam and the three girls crumpled in a heap on the ground. Everyone else was laughing, and Milly had a big smile on her face.

"I think someone has played a clever trick," said the gym teacher, Mr Lean, looking sideways at Milly. "I'll have to have a stern talk with whoever did this."

The surprising thing was that once Prunella, Beatie and
Floe had recovered they couldn't stop talking about what
had happened.

They bombarded Milly with all sorts of questions about how she had made the magic potion and how it worked.

They even invited her to sit with them at lunch. Milly was happy to be their friend, but she didn't want there to be any more nasty tricks.

So all four girls agreed only to use magic to be helpful and not for mischief.

And Milly never ever told anyone about the 'Wild Shoes' spell
and where she had found it!